THE X-TAILS
snowboard at
SHRED PARK

WRITTEN BY
L.A. Fielding

ILLUSTRATED BY
Victor Guiza

Library and Archives Canada Cataloguing in Publication

Fielding, L. A. (Lawrence Anthony), 1977-, author
Snowboard at Shred Park / written by L.A. Fielding; illustrated by Victor Guiza.

(The X tails)
ISBN 978-0-9937135-2-1 (pbk.)

I. Guiza, Victor, illustrator II. Title. III. Series: Fielding, L. A. (Lawrence Anthony), 1977- . X tails.

PS8611.I362S66 2014   jC813'.6   C2014-901463-5

Copyright © 2013 The X-tails Enterprises

The X-tails Enterprises
Prince George, BC Canada

Printed in Canada

Design and text layout by Margaret Cogswell
margaretcogswell@gmail.com

. . . .

I dedicate this book to my zoober-cool wife, Corrie, and my
two zoober-awesome kids, Colton and Dylann.

Big thanks to my family and friends who have been so supportive
and have helped to make the X-tails become a reality.

. . . .

MEET THE X-TAILS!

WISDOM

The smart and responsible lion who is the natural leader of the X-tails. He is a master at solving problems and can fix almost anything. Wisdom loves to **"ROOaaaRRRR!"** when he is having fun.

CHARM

The cute and bubbly kangaroo. She loves the spotlight and performing at contests in front of big crowds. Her kangaroo legs are perfect for jumping high and pedaling fast. When Charm is really happy, you will see her **HOP** around or **THUMP** her foot with a big smile.

CRASH

The clumsy, messy, and very goofy hippo. Crash usually finds himself in all sorts of trouble and is thankful that his X-tail friends are always there when he needs them. You can't help but laugh with Crash at the many silly things he does, especially when he bellows **"GaaaWHOOOOmPHaaaaa!"**

FLIGHT

The strong and fearless rocker gorilla. Flight not only plays the air guitar but also loves to play on any jump he can find. Although he is really big and hairy, this gorilla is a gentle giant. You know Flight is ready for air time when you hear him grunt, **"OOOHHHH, OOOHHHH, OOOHHHH!"**

Dazzle

The tough and brave bear who is a tomboy at heart. The boys have difficulty keeping up with Dazzle. And good luck trying to slow her down! She has a big grin, and you will often hear her friendly growl, **"GRRRRR!"**

MISCHIEF

The practical joker of the bunch. You know Mischief is up to something sneaky when you see his mischievous grin. He is a little short for a wolf, so be careful you don't confuse him with a fox—he doesn't like that much. But being small always works to his advantage. You will hear Mischief howl when he is excited. **"aaaaWHOOOOO!"**

And we can't forget about the X-van, which takes the X-tails to the mountains, ocean, BMX tracks, and skateboard parks. This off-road machine can go anywhere and easily fits all of the X-tails' gear. Wisdom the Lion is always the driver of the X-van.

THE X-Van

The X-tails looked and couldn't believe their eyes. He had done it again! Crash the Hippo had licked the frozen metal chairlift bar. As always, his tongue was stuck. They watched Crash stretch his slobbery tongue back and forth. Finally, there was a loud *thwack* and the foolish hippo was free.

"GaaWHOOOMPHaaaa!"

"I won't do that again," giggled Crash. The rest of the
X-tails couldn't help but laugh with their silly friend.
They were all zoober-excited because they were on
their way to snowboard at Shred Park!

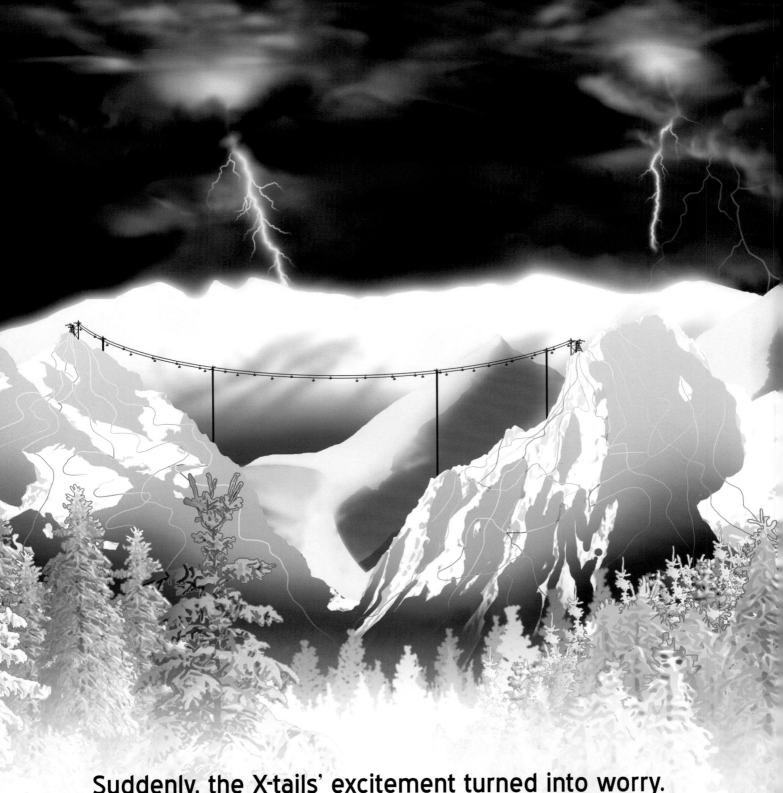

Suddenly, the X-tails' excitement turned into worry. Off in the distance, dark spooky clouds raced over the mountains straight toward them.

"Oh no," said Wisdom the Lion, "that's a snow squall!"

The storm was getting closer and closer. Wisdom realized it was worse than he had thought. "That isn't snow falling from the sky!" he yelled. "It's hail the size of baseballs!" The X-tails shrieked as the hail came closer, almost hitting them.

"Hurry," gasped Wisdom. "Pull down the bubble!" They pulled down the plastic bubble on top of the chairlift just in time.

The hail bounced noisily off the plastic and sounded like popping popcorn. Luckily for the X-tails, they were safe inside their bubble.

POP! POP! POP!

Finally, the storm passed and they were off the chairlift.

"Let's rock and roll!" grunted Flight the Gorilla. He pretended to play an electric guitar before leading his friends down the mountain.

Arriving at Shred Park, the X-tails **HOPPED** into the air with excitement!

The tricks they did
were zoober-amazing:

RODEO

FRONT
FLIP

Cannonball

and a

Switch Boardslide.

The X-tails were unstoppable!

They zipped to the bottom and then took a chairlift back to the top.

The X-tails were about to do another run through Shred Park when Flight the Gorilla spoke up.

"Hey, who's that over there?"

They looked at each other and shrugged their shoulders.

"I've never seen that elephant before," said Mischief the Wolf quietly.

"Why don't we invite the elephant to snowboard with us?" suggested Flight.

"No, we don't know him," answered Mischief.

That's when Wisdom the Lion spoke up. "Mischief, don't you remember when you first met us? You were all by yourself, and we invited you to come skateboarding. Do you remember how that made you feel?"

"That made me feel good," said Mischief. "I'm glad you asked me to skateboard with you, because now we're all friends. Yeah, let's invite the elephant to snowboard with us."

"Hey, Dude," said Flight the Gorilla
to the mysterious elephant.

"Are you speaking to me?" asked the elephant.

"Yes," said Flight. "Why are you sitting all by yourself and not shredding the park? You should snowboard with us. We're the X-tails. What's your name?"

"My name is Pride," said the elephant. "Are you sure you want to snowboard with me? Everyone says that I'm too big to snowboard and they make fun of my size."

"That's terrible that others make fun of you," said Flight. "We're all different shapes and sizes, and that's what makes us all special."

Thinking for a few seconds, Flight smiled and said, "Our big size helps us get speed. Plus, you have a cool trunk on your face, so you can invent new snowboard tricks. You could invent a *Trunk-plant* in the superpipe. You're lucky to be an elephant!"

"Wow, I never thought of myself that way," said Pride. "You're right, I am special. I would love to snowboard with all of you. I've always dreamed of becoming a really good snowboarder."

"**aaaaWHOOOOO!**" howled Mischief the Wolf with a toothy grin. "Well, what are we waiting for? Let's hit the jumps! You go first, Pride, and we'll watch."

With a feeling of belonging and happiness, Pride the Elephant headed for the first jump. Pride picked up speed—lots and lots of speed.

EXPERT ONLY

"GRRRRR!"

Dazzle gritted her teeth with worry. "This is not going to be pretty. Even though I'm a bear, I can't bear to watch."

As Pride soared off the big jump, his board and feet shot straight toward the sky. As quickly as he flew into the air, he just as quickly fell onto the hard snow, landing with a loud *thud*.

The X-tails zoomed down on their snowboards
to make sure their new friend was not hurt.

"Are you okay?" asked Wisdom.

"Yes, I'm just embarrassed," said Pride. "I wanted to
impress all of you."

"Falling is how everyone learns," said Wisdom. "You must go at your own pace and imagine the trick in your head before you try it. Trust me, you'll be shredding on your snowboard before you know it. I'm sure you'll even be doing *Trunk-plants* in the superpipe."

Pride smiled. "I'm not going to give up!" he said as he jumped up on his snowboard.

Pride stood still for a moment, not moving or saying anything.

"Did you fall asleep with your eyes open?" asked Crash the Hippo.

Pride laughed. "Nope, I just landed a *Three-sixty* in my head. Now it's time to do it in real life." He pointed his board straight down for the next jump.

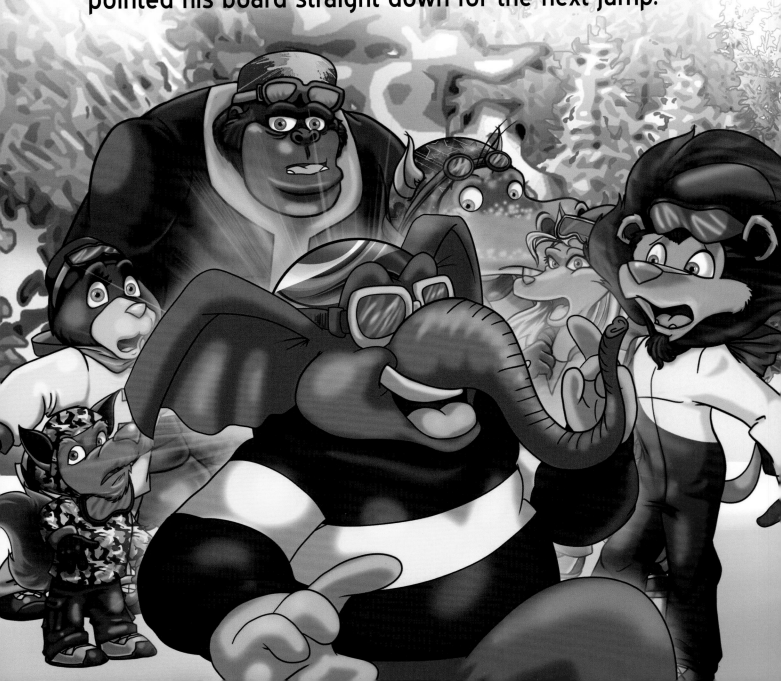

Dazzle covered her eyes again. "I still can't bear to watch," she cringed.

Pride tucked low toward the jump. His snowboard hummed with speed and snow shot out from behind him. He sailed off the jump.

And do you know what happened?

Pride's board and body turned so slowly that the X-tails did not think he was going to land his trick; but at the last second, Pride did it!

He landed a perfect *Three-sixty!*

"ROOaaaRRRR!"

boomed Wisdom the Lion. "That was zoober-cool!" The X-tails cheered and then rode down to congratulate their new friend.

"We all knew you could do it, Pride!" said Charm the Kangaroo.

"Are you sure you ALL knew I could do it?" asked Pride.

"Uh huh," they nodded.

"Well, that's funny," said Pride. "In the middle of my trick, I thought I saw Dazzle covering her eyes."

Dazzle the Bear smirked. "Okay, maybe I was a teeny weeny bit worried."

The X-tails and Pride laughed so hard that their bellies hurt.

After that day, the X-tails lost contact with Pride.
It was three years later when Flight the Gorilla came
home one day and said, "Guess who I just saw at
the grocery store?"

"Who?" asked the X-tails curiously.

"I saw Pride the Elephant," said Flight.
"And that's not all . . . I got his autograph!"

"What do you mean . . . autograph?" they asked.

"Pride is now a professional snowboarder!" said Flight excitedly. He whipped out a copy of *Zoo Snowboard* magazine and there was Pride on the front cover. "Look," said Flight, "he's doing a *Trunk-plant* in the superpipe!"

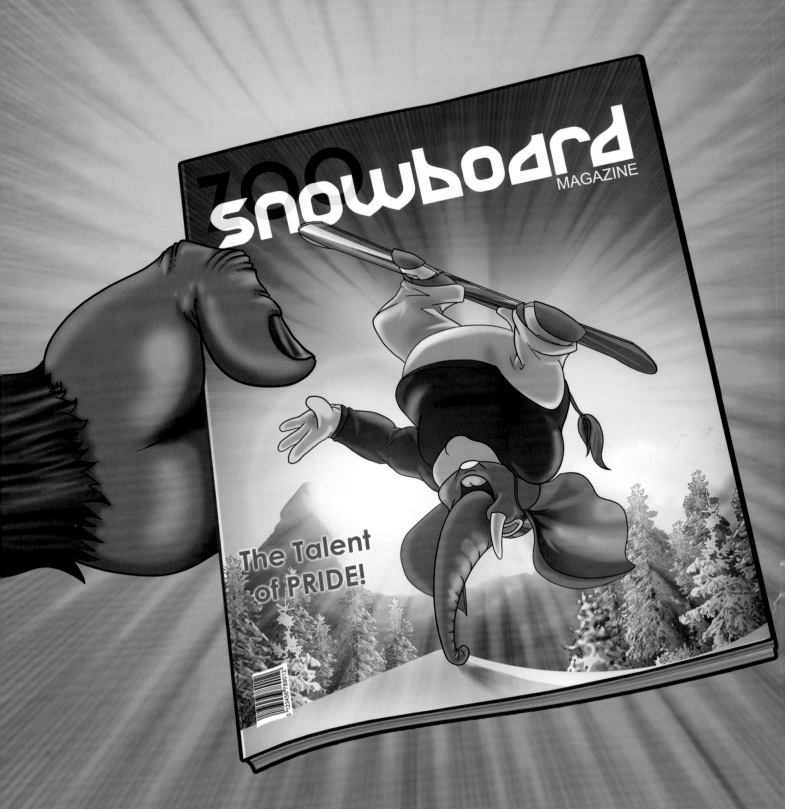

The X-tails grinned and high-fived each other. "Wow," said Dazzle, "he never gave up. Now he's a professional snowboarder and we're the ones who gave him his first lesson!"

"Yeah," said Wisdom, "he just had to believe in himself. I sure am proud of Pride!"

THe enD

THE TRICK-TIONARY

BUTTER

No air time required for this trick. Leaning forward or backward, the snowboarder lifts up the nose or tail of the snowboard while sliding and spinning along the ground. Crash the Hippo not only likes butter on his popcorn but also loves to butter on his snowboard.

CANNONBALL

A high-flying trick where the snowboarder grabs the nose and tail of the snowboard at the same time. Long arms sure help with this trick, and that's why Flight the Gorilla is the only X-tail to ever land it.

FRONT FLIP

A flip performed in a forward motion where the snowboarder rotates upside down. Charm has mastered this trick because of her kangaroo jumping power.

HAND-PLANT

Balancing on one hand upside down on top of the wall in a halfpipe, superpipe, or quarterpipe. This trick is very similar to the Trunk-plant, which was first invented by Pride the Elephant. The Trunk-plant is even more difficult than the Hand-plant because the trunk is used to hold up the weight of an elephant, which requires great strength and balance.

MCTWIST

A zoober-cool air performed in a halfpipe, superpipe, or quarterpipe, which involves spinning one and a half rotations. During the spin, a flip is thrown and the snowboarder lands riding forward. This trick was first invented on a skateboard and is a favorite of Mischief the Wolf in the Shred Park or the skateboard park.

RODEO

This trick involves spinning one and a half rotations while soaring like a bird. During the spin, a flip is thrown and the snowboarder lands riding backward. Crash the Hippo learned this trick by accident when his helmet slipped over his eyes and he was unable to see while flying through the air. Crash ended up landing it! He has been able to do this trick ever since, but only when he closes his eyes.

SWITCH BOARDSLIDE

Sliding the snowboard sideways on top of a metal rail or box. To perform this trick "switch," the snowboarder must ride backward up to the rail or box. Be careful—rails and boxes can be very slippery!

THREE-SIXTY

A trick that can be performed on big or small jumps, which involves spinning one full rotation. After you learn the Three-sixty, ask Wisdom the Lion to teach you to spin two full rotations for a Seven-twenty.

TRIPLE CORK

Completion of three flips while spinning several rotations through the air. Out of all the X-tails, only Dazzle the Bear has landed this trick. Courage and lots of practice are required.

WILDCAT

A flip performed in a backward cartwheel motion with the snowboarder rotating upside down. Completing two Wildcats in the air is called a Supercat. This trick is Wisdom the Lion's favorite.

L.A. FIELDING

is an author of children's literature and a member of the Canadian Authors Association. He dreamed up the X-tails for his two children, while telling stories on their long distance trips to the mountains each winter weekend. It is his family's cozy log home in Prince George, British Columbia, and their Fielding Shred Shack at a local ski resort, where he draws his inspiration.

Growing up skateboarding, biking, and snowboarding, L.A. Fielding now shares the fun of those sports with his family. When not writing or telling stories, he focuses his thoughts on forestry as a Registered Professional Forester. *The X-tails Snowboard at Shred Park* is the first published book in the X-tails series.

Other books in the series include:

- *The X-tails Skateboard at Monster Ramp*
- *The X-tails Ski at Spider Ridge*
- *The X-tails BMX at Thunder Track*
- *The X-tails Surf at Shark Bay*
- *The X-tails Travel to the Jamboree Jam*
- *The X-tails Dirt Bike at Badlands*

CHECK OUT  AT WWW.THEXTAILS.COM